**W9-DJI-271**

101 FUN CONNECT THE DOTS

This book belongs to:

_____

This book is filled with 101 amazing dot to dot puzzles for hours of fun! The puzzles are separated into 3 levels; ranging from easy to challenging!

This book features:
- 101 FUN CONNECT THE DOT PUZZLES
- COLOR-IN IMAGES AFTER COMPLETION
- LARGE SIZE PAGES
- 3 PROGRESSIVE LEVELS
- COMPLETION CERTIFICATE IN THE END

For the Parent

Dot to dot puzzles help your child to learn how to count numbers and develop fine motor skills by tracing the lines. Continued practice improves hand-eye coordination and helps to improve your kids dexterity and muscle memory through drawing a line and following the dots to complete the image.

Dot to dot activities also helps to nurture the development of your child's brain and improves visualization skills, thought processes, problem solving skills and emotional intelligence.

Level 1 - Simple Dot to Dot

Let's start with some simple dot to dot puzzles.

Ready? Let's go!

Mommy Duck

My First Bike

Bike

Little Chicks

Dolphin Splashes

The Long Leg Bird

The Aardvark

The Smiley Car

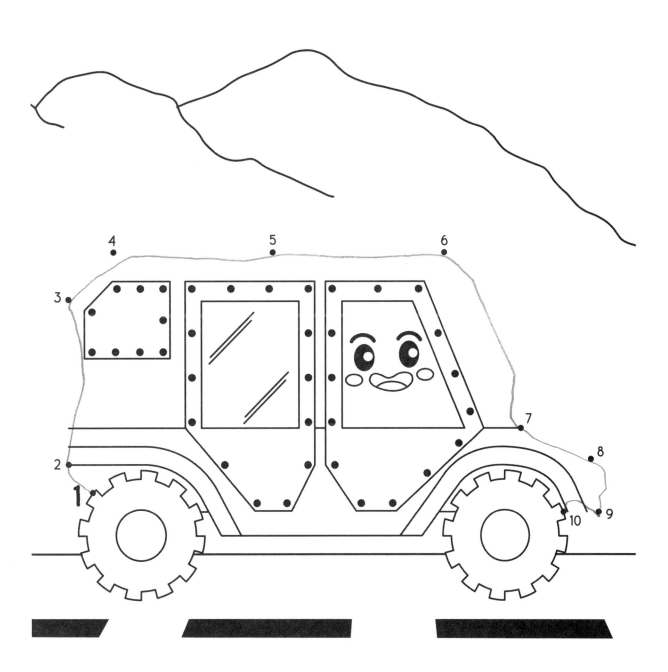

School Bus Goes Around Town

SCHOOL BUS

The Banana Boat on the Beach

The Bear

The Christmas Wreath For You

Christmas Bell

Grandma's Flower Vase

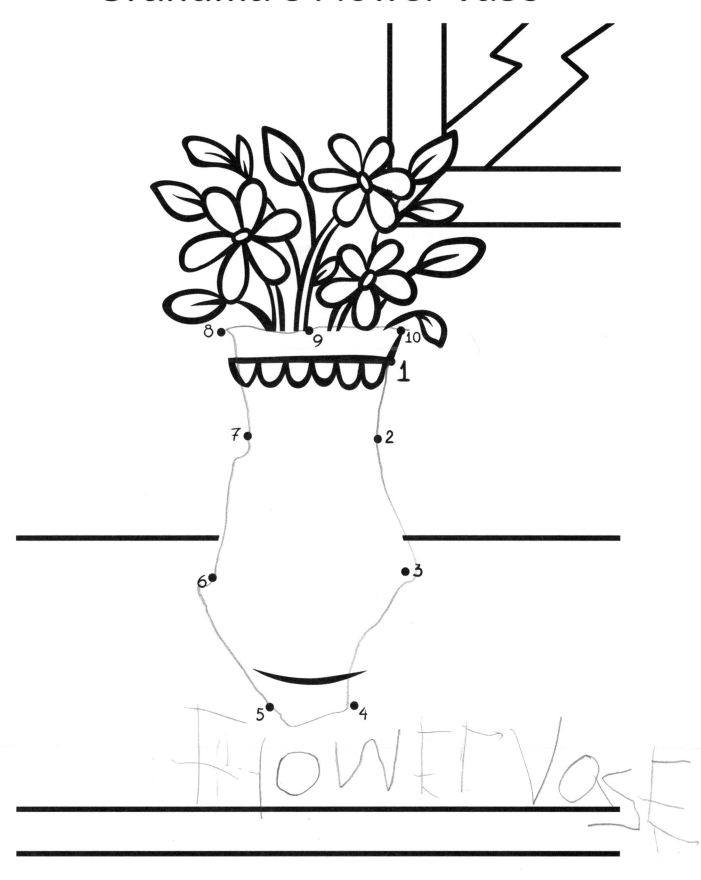

The Globe Teaches Me The World!

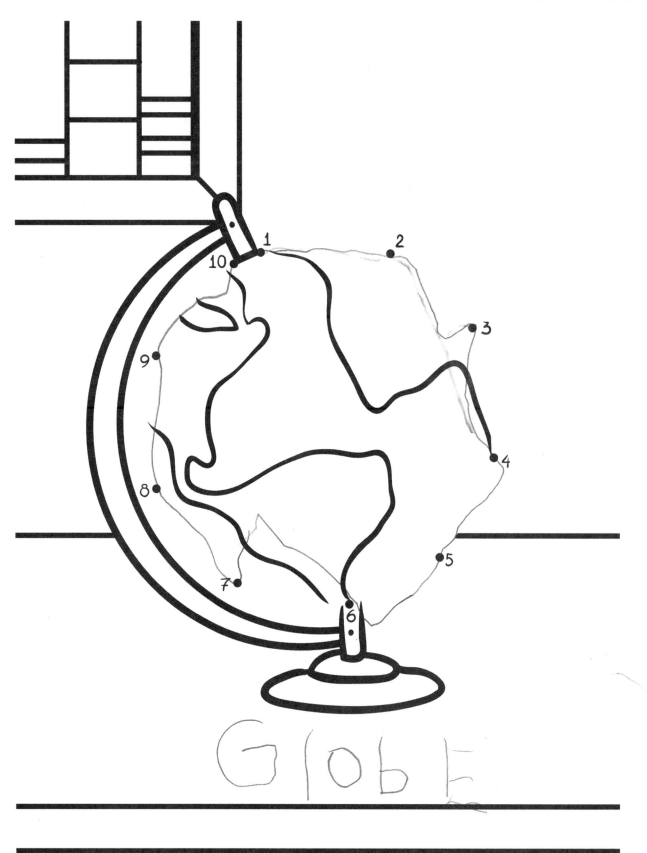

Happy Easter Bunny

The Paint Palette

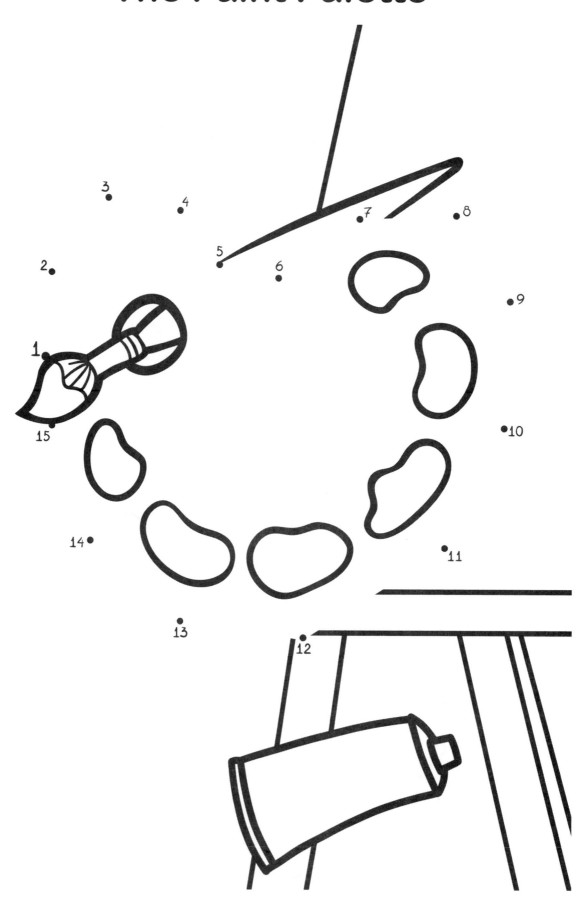

The Candle Light

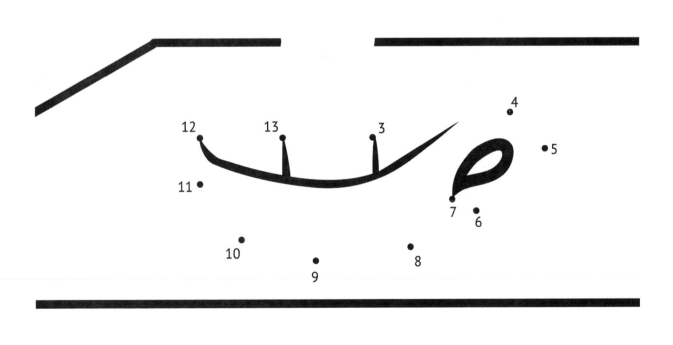

Hedgehog Goes to Find His Friend

Little Chick Goes on a Trip

Wink Back at the Penguin!

My Fish Friend

Sleeping Mushroom

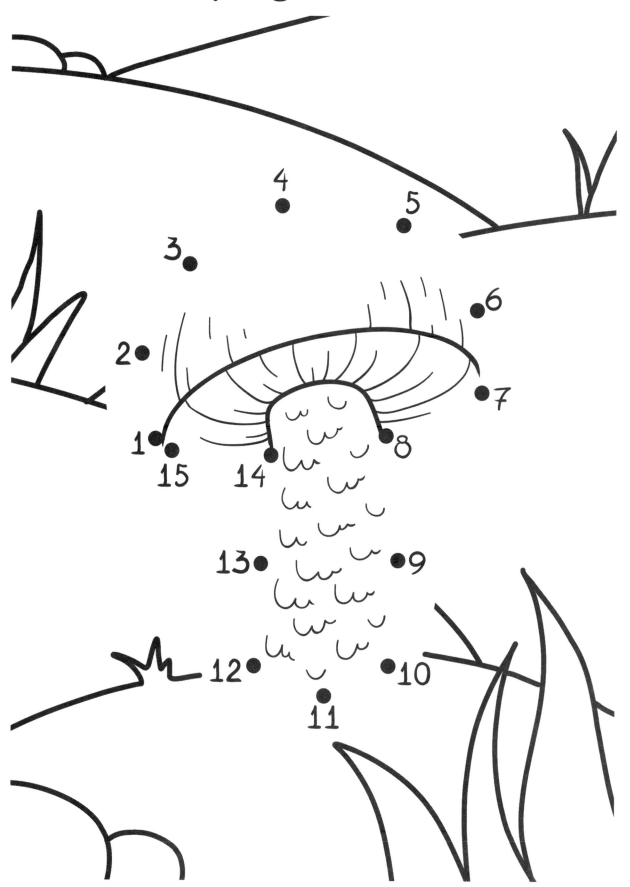

The Pirate Hat

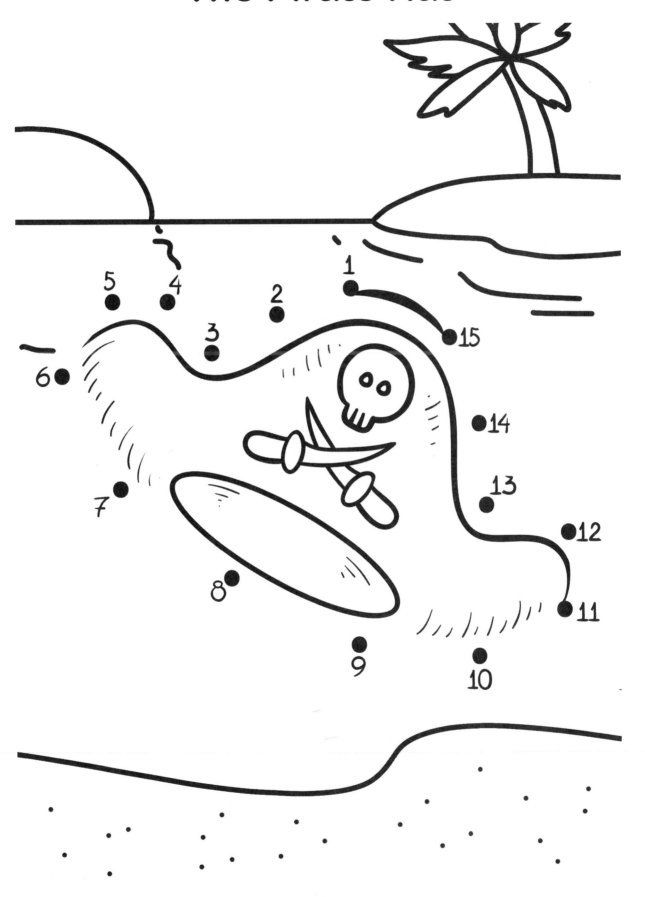

My Treasure Map

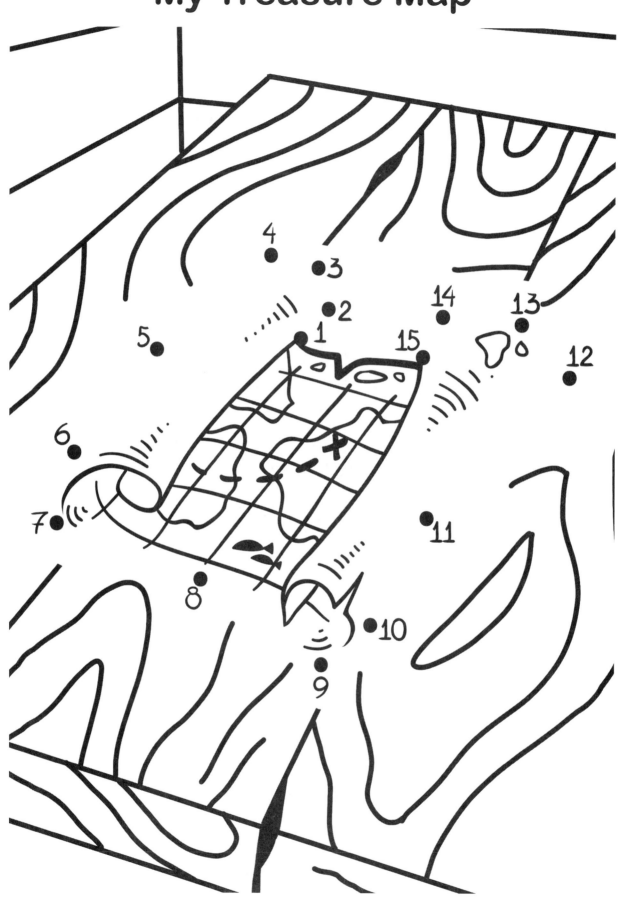

Rubber Boots

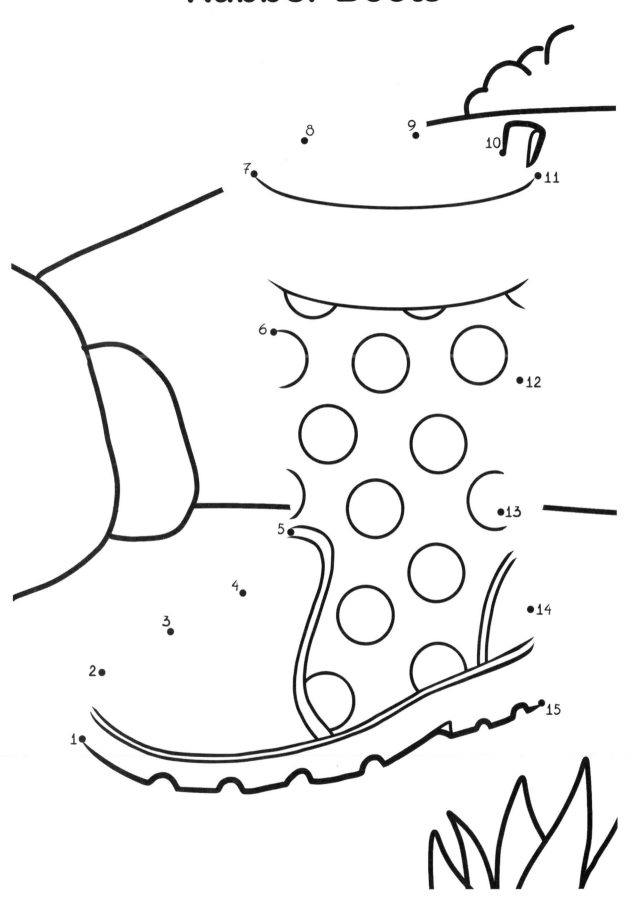

Toothpaste Makes My Teeth Clean

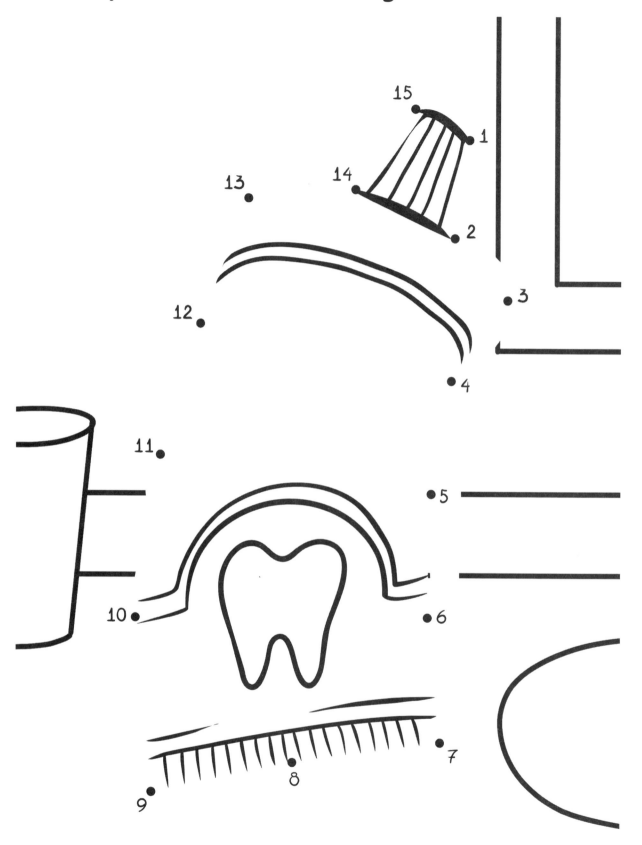

Mom's Flower Hat

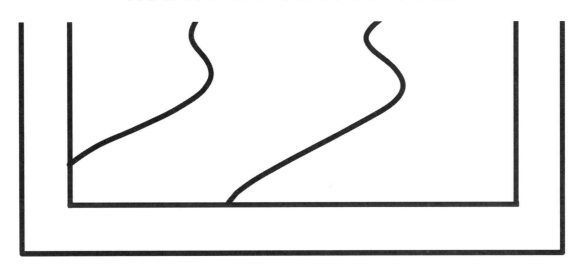

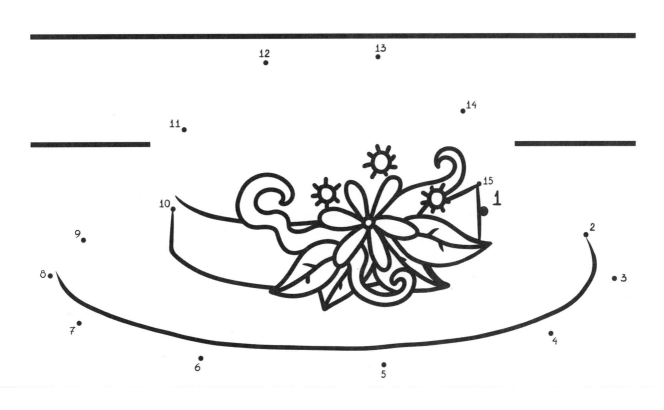

Brother's Summer Pants

The Night Stand Table

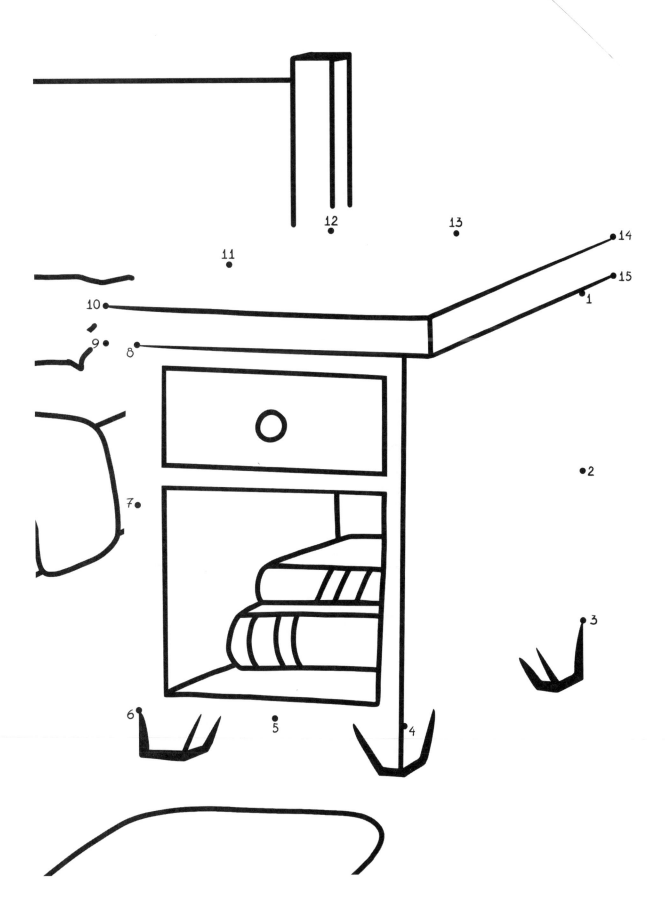

Juice Box Snack

Level 2 - Challenging Dot to Dot

Great job! You are amazing!

Let's continue with more dot to dot!

The Little Sheep

The Car Honk Goes Beep Beep

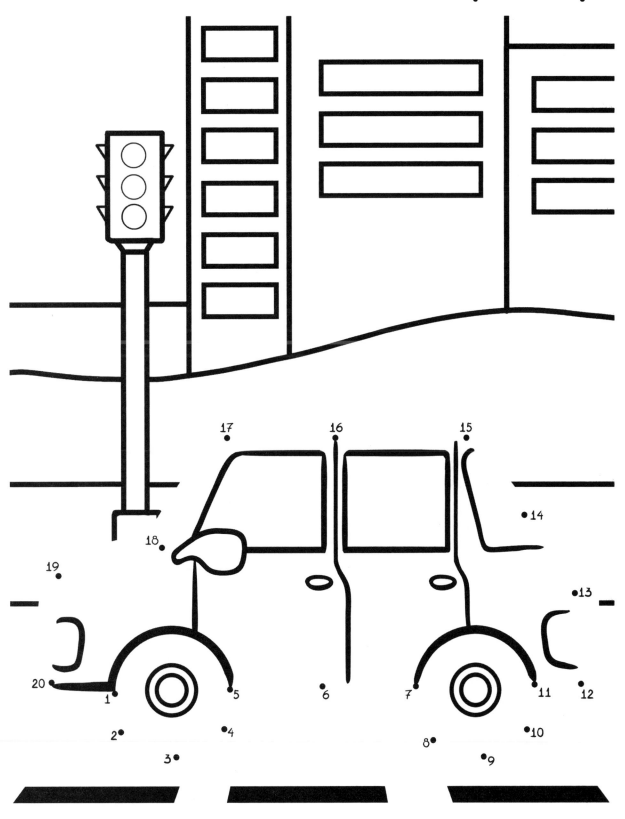

Happy Bear

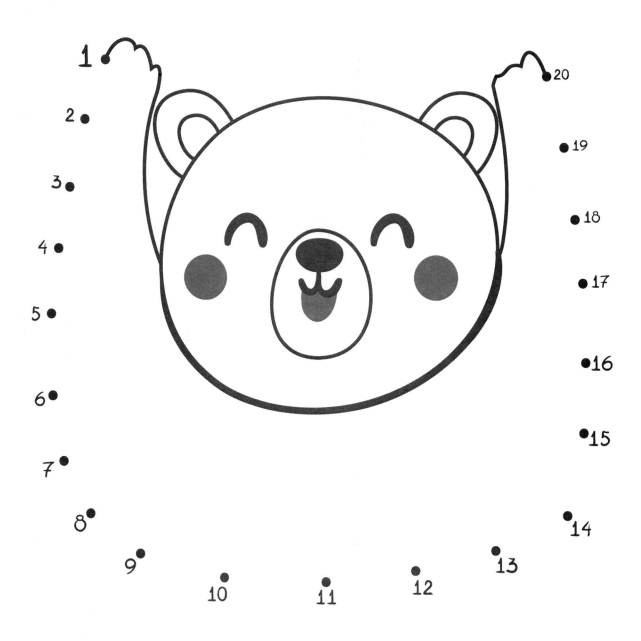

The Pony

Mr. Slow

20 1

14
13 15 18 19 2
12 3
16 17 4
11 5
10 8 7 6
9

38

Snowman Ornament

That Delicious Peach

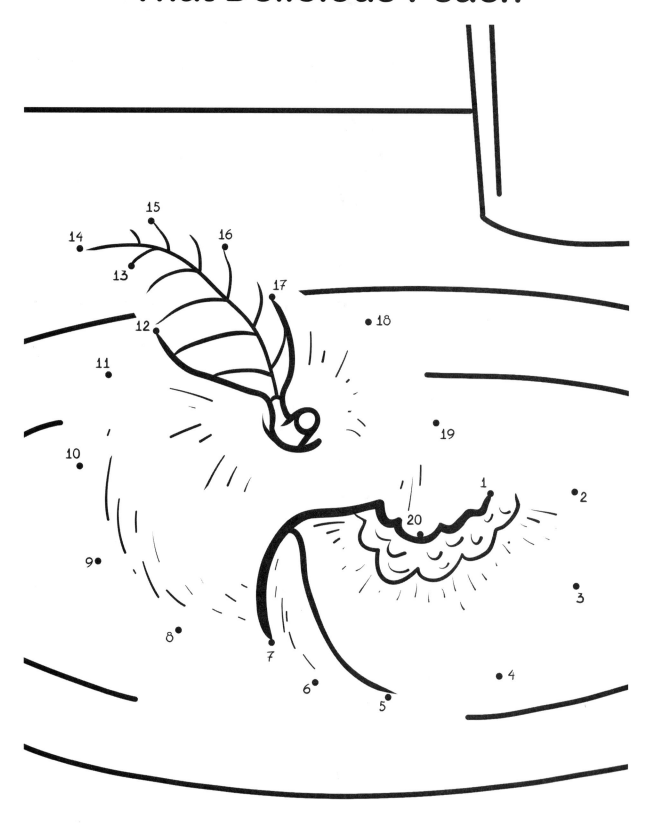

Is It Time For Ice Cream?

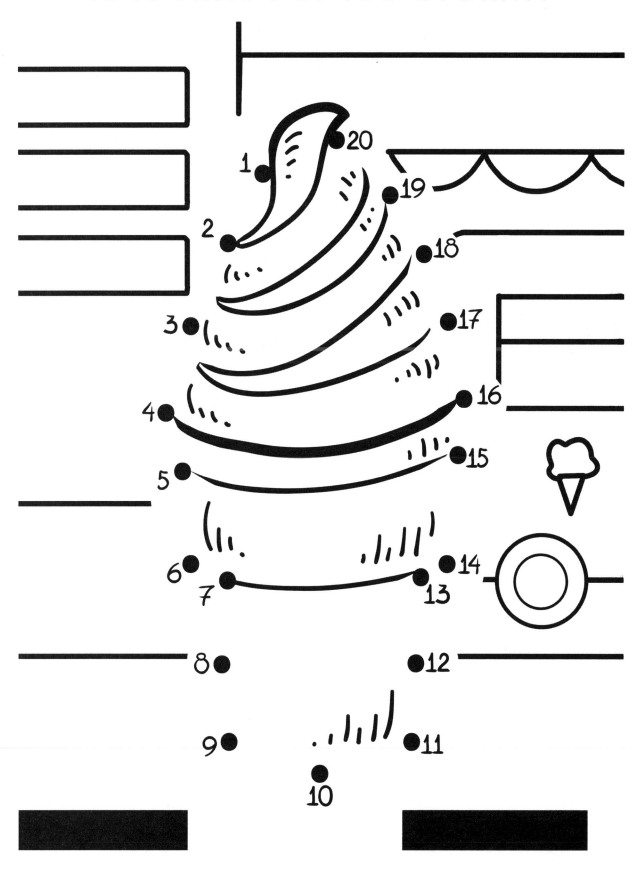

Have You Got an Easel?

Zebra in the Wild

The Lion Cub

Grandpa's Delicious Pie

My First Kick Scooter

Sweet Rabbit

Short Sleeve Shirt

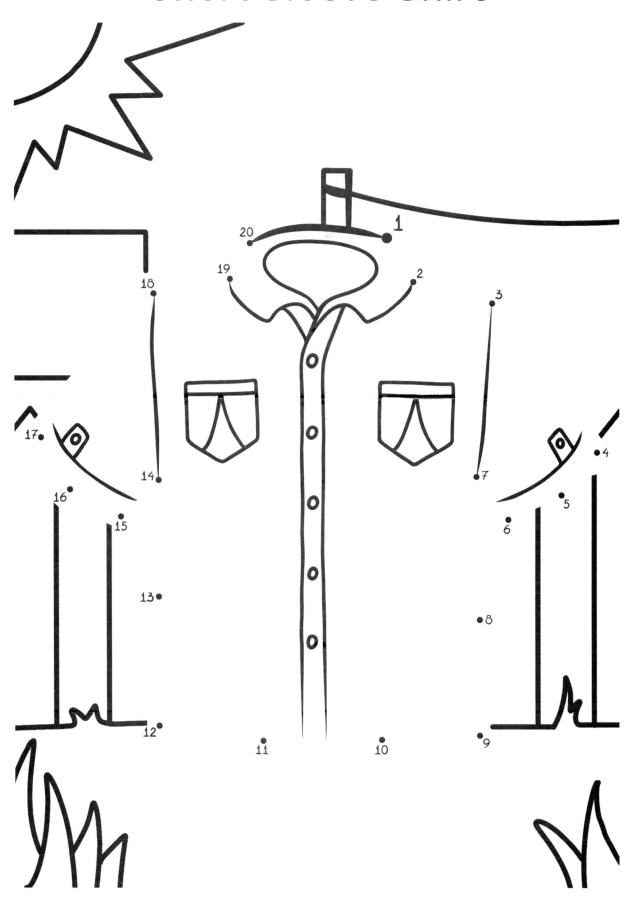

A Chips Bag

I Am A Little Tea Pot!

That Adorable Beaver

Puppy Winks

Do We Have Stew For Dinner?

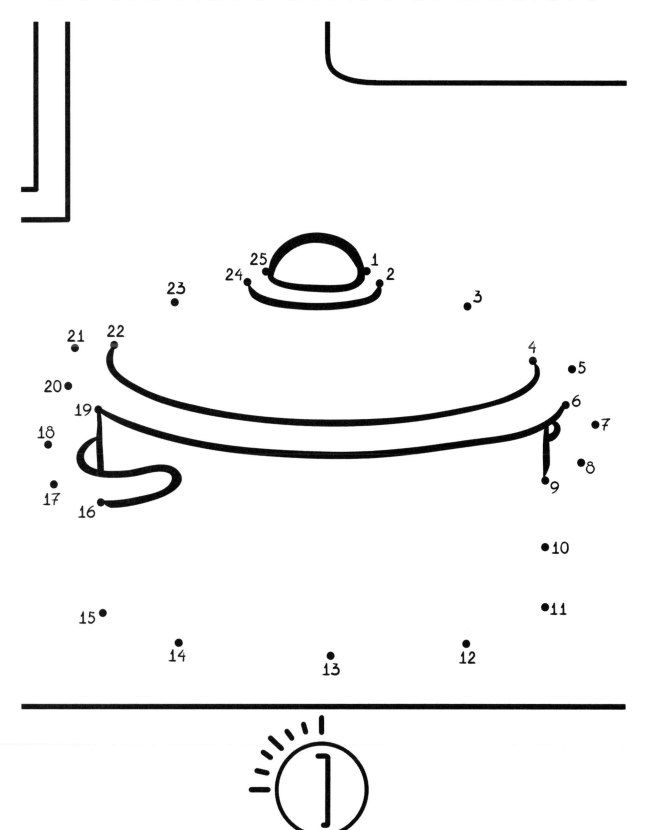

Lady Bug

A Shooting Star

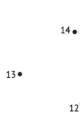

21 22

25
24   1

19
20   23   2
                      4
15   3
17
16   18   6
                          7
14

13
12
          10   9

11

Suitcase For Traveling

Happy Fox

That Burger!

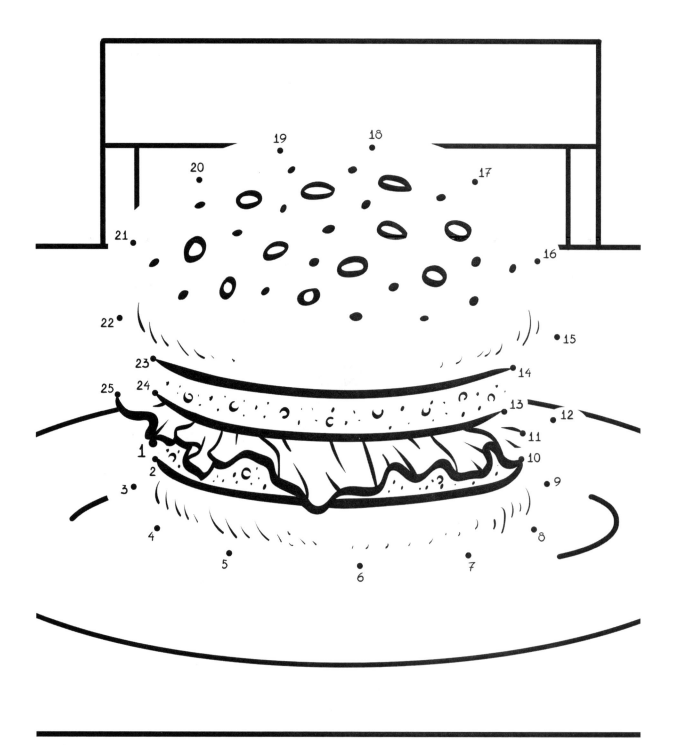

Friendly Hamster

A Rubber Duck or a Real Duck?

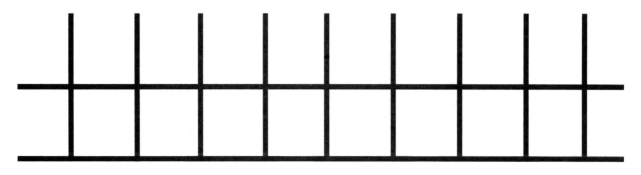

What Kind of Fish is this?

A Lion That Has a Lot of Hair

Busy Bee

Level 3 - Advanced Dot to Dot

Well done! You are doing wonderful!

This is the last level with the most complicated dot to dot. Let's see if you can solve them. You're almost there!

Cupcake with A Lemon Slice

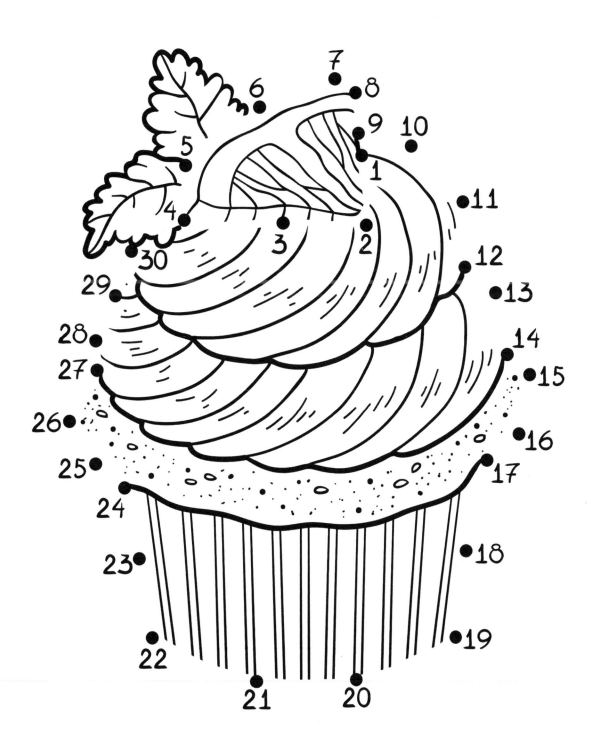

Little Frog

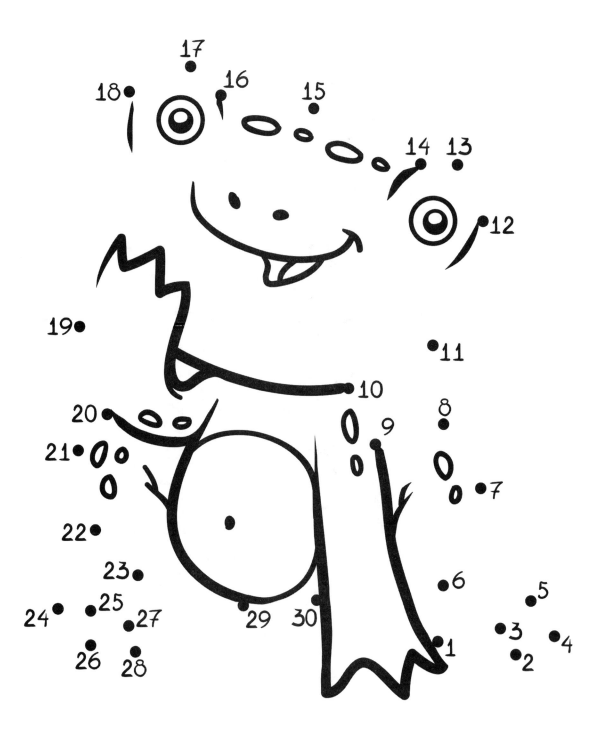

The Scary Cobra

Spinach is Not My Favorite

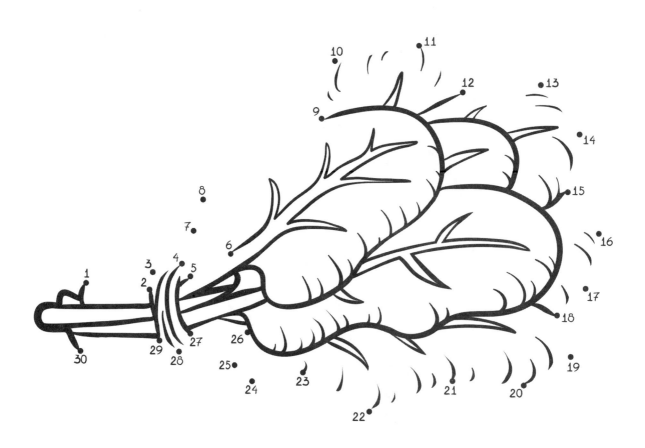

The Seahorse

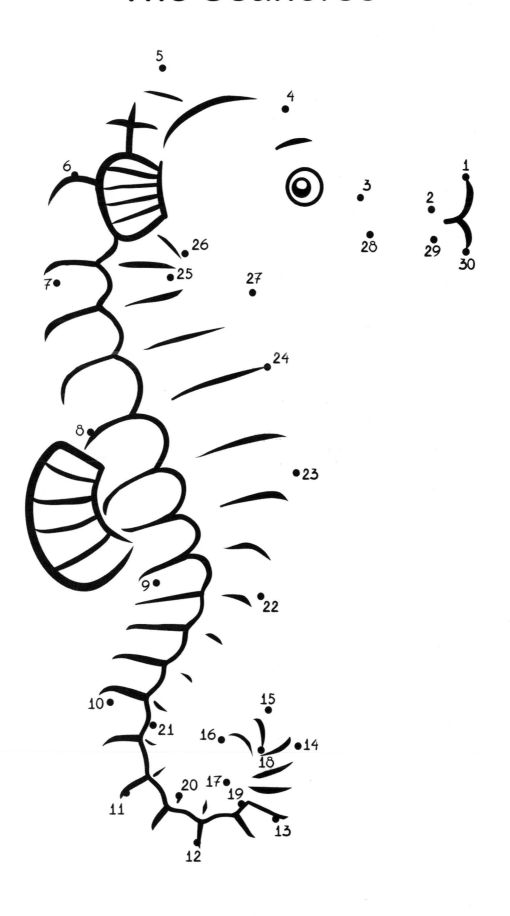

The Walrus

A Loaf of Bread

Snorkel Mask

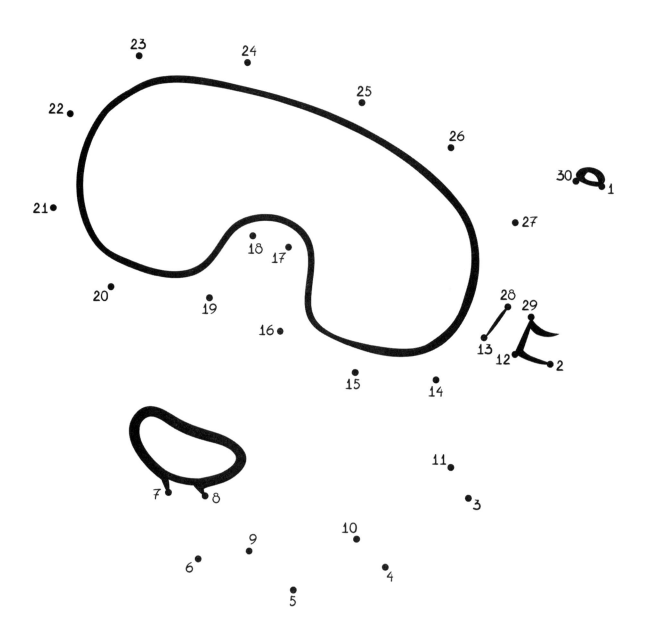

Little Octopus

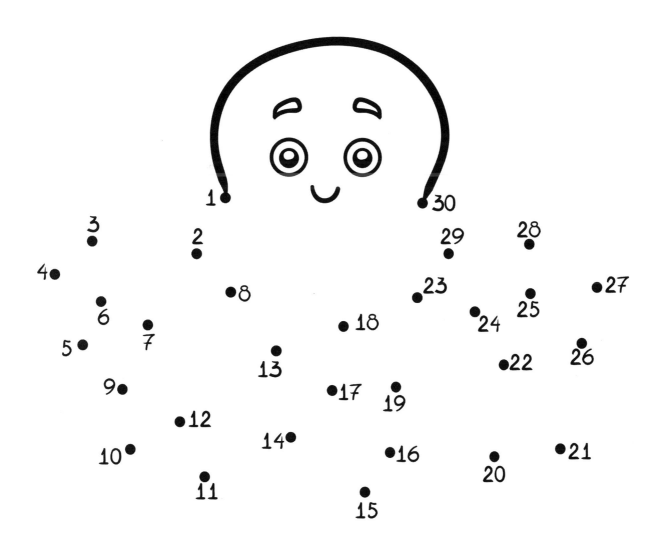

What Type of Rhino Is Extinct?

The Piggie Family

Dad's Favorite Guitar

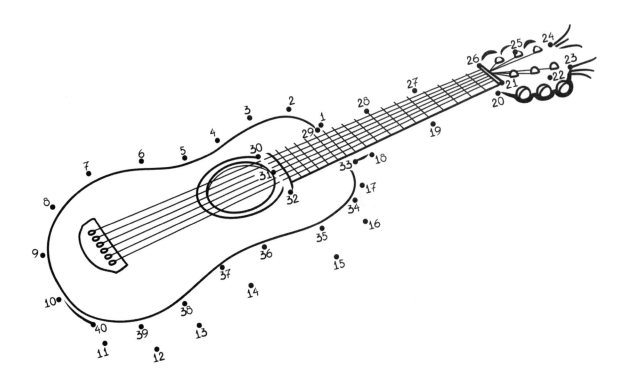

The Cartoon Mouse

Kangaroos Are From Australia

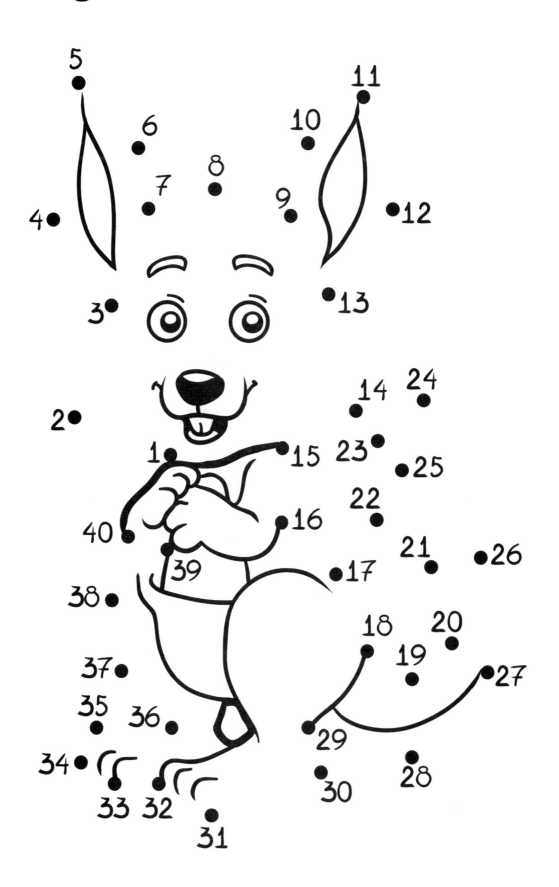

Palm Tree

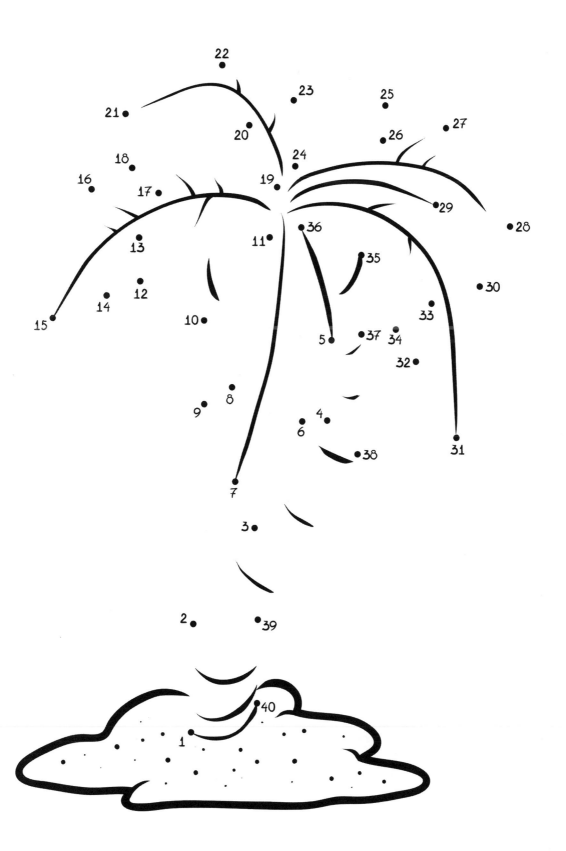

The Awesome Peacock

The Adorable Sheep

It's a Lynx!

The Polar Bear

Two Giraffe Friends

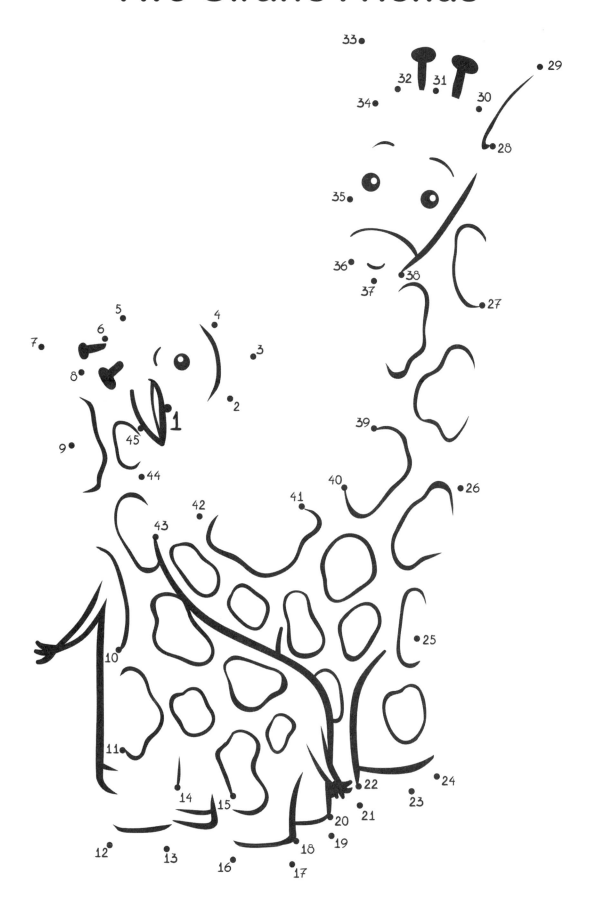

The Yak

The Numbat

Mr. Squirrel

The Proud Dog

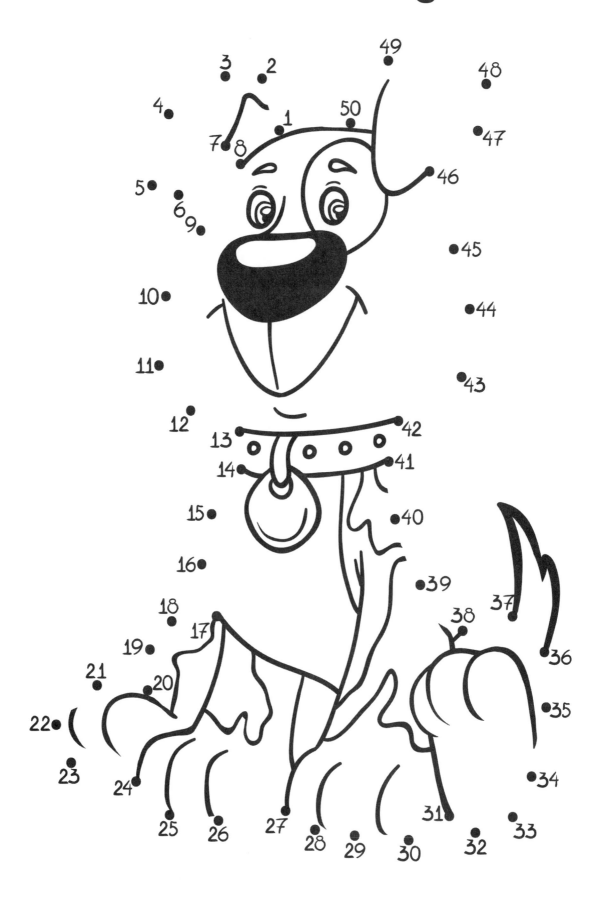

Mrs. Rabbit

Beautiful Deer

The Standing Tiger

Mommy and Baby Giraffe

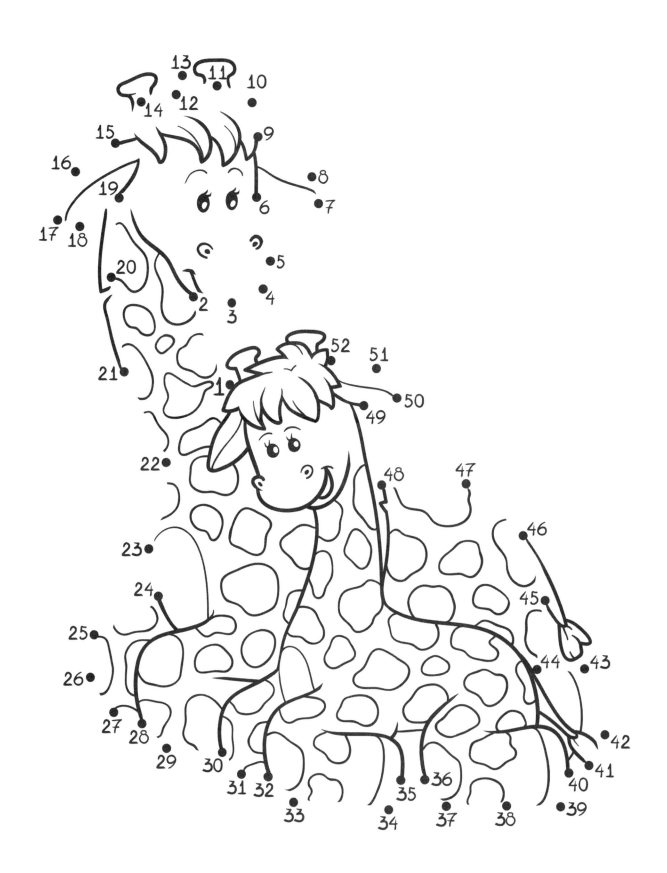

Raccoon and Its Food!

Black Currants

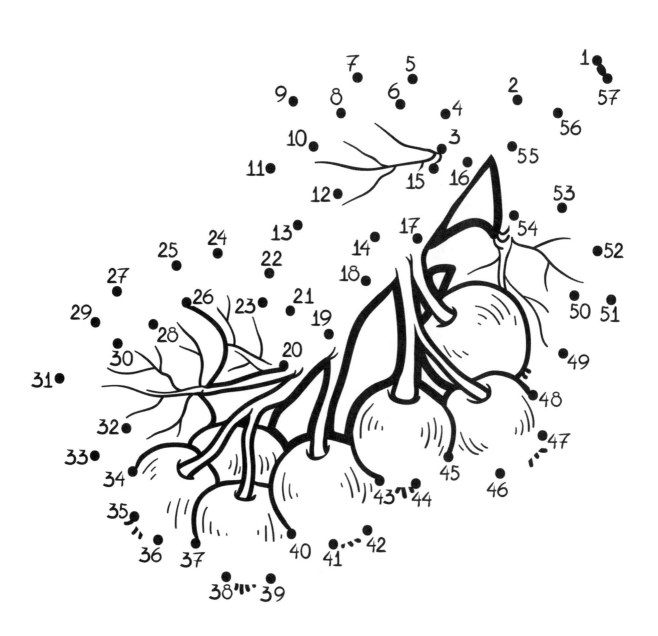

94

Bonus Level – Complex Dot to Dot

What? Really? You want even more? Remarkable!

Alright, that's the most we can do. After that, we give up. You won!

Holly Branch

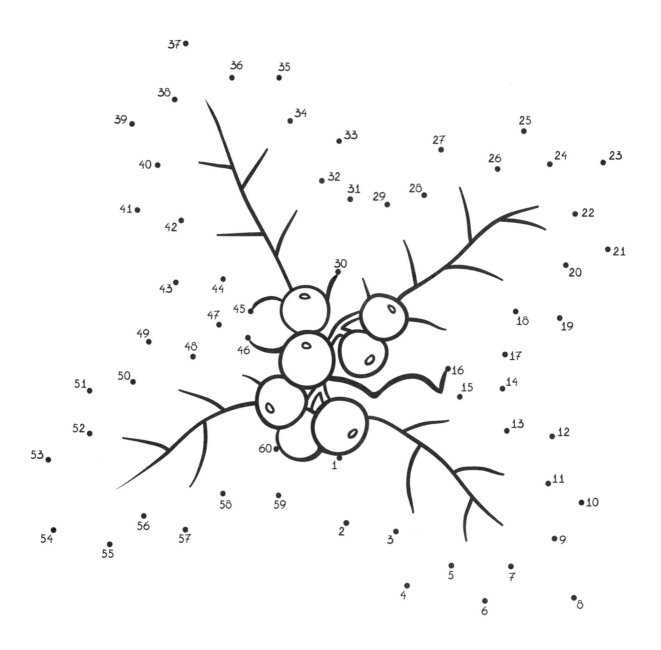

Majestic Deer

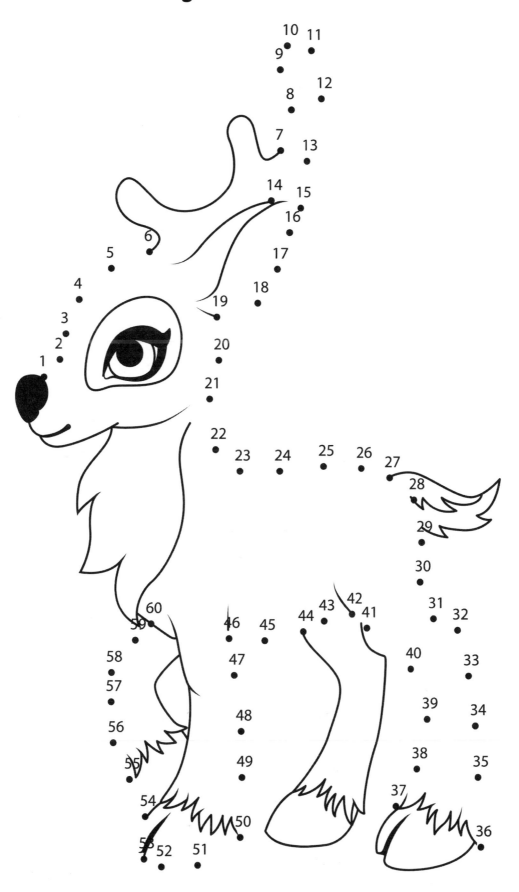

The Two-Humps Camel

It's Santa Claus

The Bear found the Honey Pot

The Goat

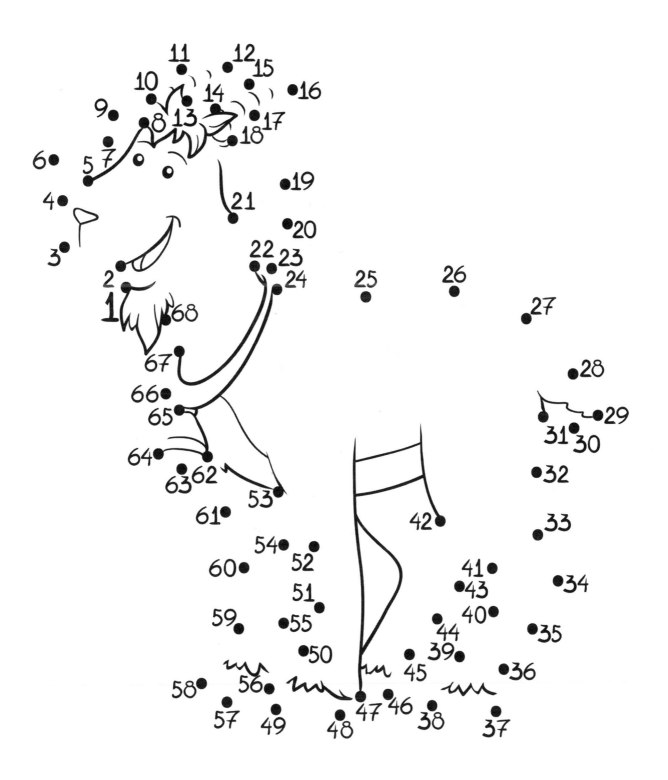

The Violin

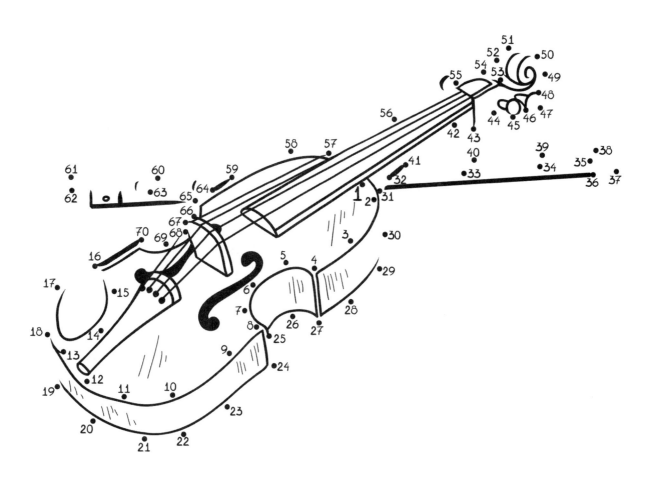

Three Monkeys!

The Calendula Flower

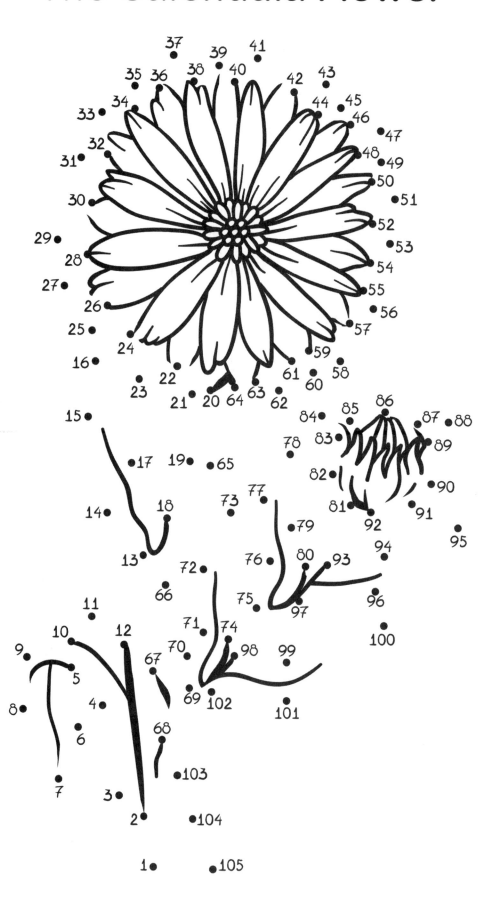

Chamomile

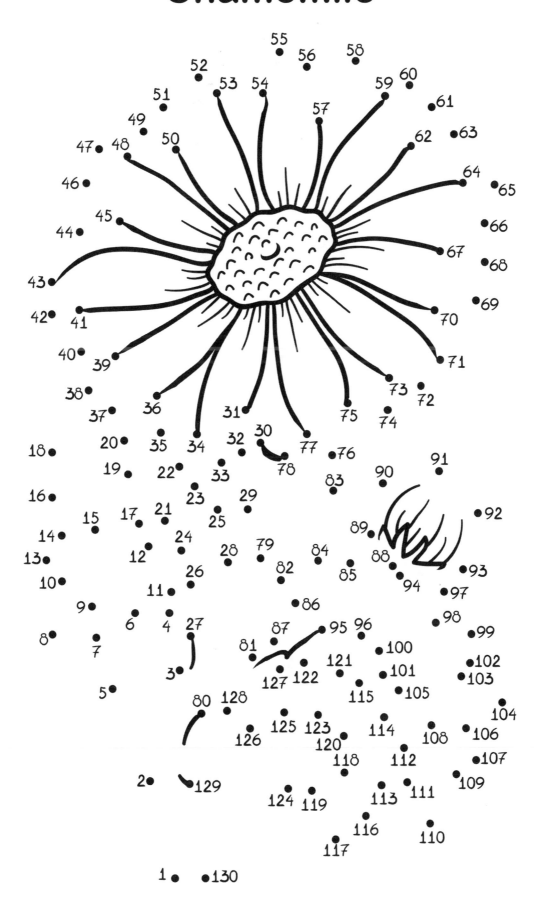

The Elephant

CONGRATULATIONS!

Great job! You did so well! If you want to continue with some more connect the dot activities, just send me an email at hello.jennifer.trace@gmail.com, I will send you some printable dot to dot puzzles for free.

My name is Jennifer Trace and I hope you enjoyed solving these puzzles. I sure enjoyed creating them. If you have any suggestions about how to improve this book, changes to make or how to make it more useful, please let me know.

If you liked this book, would you be so kind and leave me a review on Amazon.

Thank you very much!
Jennifer Trace

Congratulations
Dot to Dot Super Star:

THE BEST!

_____

Date:_____   Signed:_____